THE
WEDDING
VIRUS

and other snippets

natalie shell

ISBN-13: 978-1511520546

Cover design by Ronit Peled and Sharon Mass / The Art of Branding
Internal design by Alicia Freile / Tango Media
Editing by Keren Peled

This book is typeset in Palatino and Futura BT.

www.theweddingvirus.com

To my girlfriends everywhere.
You know who you are.

And to my Mr.
You know who you are, too.

CONTENTS

INTRODUCTION

SCRIBBLES ABOUT WOMEN

DATING

SEX

ENGAGEMENT

THE WEDDING

INTRODUCTION

"Everyone lies.
Or they have
amnesia."

"A real relationship is the ultimate fantasy."

Beurre & Sel

There's only one thing more delicious to me than cookie dough.

And that's the taste of beaten butter and sugar, just before you put the eggs in.

I know, I know, it sounds disgusting maybe. But doesn't everyone have weird loves like this?

I thought you may have preferred it if I was writing about baking. Maybe we should all go have some Nutella on a spoon.

Even the universe is against me.

I had a crap night due to a bad, sad, conversation with boyfriend-who-doesn't-want-to-get-married.

No, I don't want to talk about it. I am working through it and can't talk about it right now.

Meanwhile, I had resigned to throw myself into work. Which worked for ten hours. . . . Until I got home and remembered we had a wedding tonight.

I caught a ride with friends from work and had barely gotten in the car before someone asked me if I was engaged - and I'm not even at the wedding yet.

Oh, the universe and signs . . .

The Wedding Virus

I'm in a café, waving my hand in my soon-to-be-married friend's face.

"I've caught the wedding virus," I say.

"It's OK to admit that, darling, most of us catch it eventually."

"No, I mean literally. There is a thing growing on my left finger. . . ."

I thrust my finger closer to her face.

"On my wedding finger!!

"And I have to have it lasered off!

"What the fuck?"

And she looks at me and starts laughing hysterically. And I'm joining in.

"This needs to be in a movie," she says, shaking her head.

Be careful what you say, people.

I've been joking about the wedding virus (followed closely by the baby epidemic).

I made it up as a concept. You know, to explain how suddenly weddings and kids spread.

It's especially contagious in groups of couples.

At least, I thought I made it up...

Oh, and believe me, I'm a stereotype.

Soon to be thirty. Living with my boyfriend of two years.

No ring. Having spent two years not once mentioning, forget pleading or begging or announcing my need to get married . . . a need I didn't have.

Suddenly wanting it.

And now frustrated at his lack of interest.

The fact that he has an ex-wife and therefore presumably knows full well how to propose isn't helping.

And I'm sitting here.

With. A. VIRUS. On. My. Wedding. Finger.

That needs to be taken off.

With a laser.

What have I become?

Who is this person?

What happened to all the stories they fed me about the man on one knee?

Of him or you or you both knowing and spontaneously getting it together?

"Obviously you've ignored all the other stories," my friend cuts in.

She reminds me of her year of torture convincing her boyfriend of eight years that they should get married. And the story of our other friend who lived with a guy for two and a half years only to break up when he announced to our Manhattan-born-and-raised-senior-associate-lawyer-at-top-firm friend that actually he had always imagined she would want to just have babies, move back to his small hick home town and be friends with the wives of his friends, and did she really want to work?

Only to find out via Facebook that he was engaged six weeks later. And married within three months.

"Do you know what my cousin told me the other day?" I interrupt.

"*'We don't wait, darling. We force.'*"

"Oh, everyone knows that," she says.

"What?" I'm still holding up my finger.

"Huh? No-one told me.

"Where's the romance in that?"

"Oh, there isn't any. Not for most people. Not really."

"Um, my parents."

"So your parents are one in a million, darling. But that's not most people's story.

"Most people beg. Cry. Scream.

"No guy really wants to get married."

It's not true, I want to yell. It can't be.

"I know guys who propose. They've always told me. I was always the girl they told.

My best guy friend proposed to his girlfriend.

OK, so what if his girlfriend told him she expected to get married that year? She also told me.

Heck, she told the butcher.

"But the point," I said to my friend, "is that he

proposed."

"Darling, his wife informed him and the whole known universe that she expected to be married. And she repeated it and repeated it and repeated it.

"Until he understood there was no way out. Unless he actually wanted out of the relationship. Which most guys don't want. Because the reason they don't propose in the first place is because they don't want anything to change. They want everything to stay the same. Always. Think of their favorite underwear or t-shirt that they can't bear to part with . . ."

I shake my head and bang it on the café's table.

"This can't really be the way it works, can it?"

"The way I see it," she says, "you have two choices. Well three, really.

"You tell him you need to get married and then you either do, or break up."

"You said three."

"The third is you accept that he doesn't want to get married. And you are OK with that."

"That's all you have for three?"

Argh.
I've caught the wedding virus!

Hors d'oeuvre

Dreams.

Somewhere in the world a girl was born who grew up to dream of white fluffy dresses that gently skimmed the floor as she danced around the room . . . and kissed her handsome prince. Or knight. Or gorgeous boy. Or delicious man. Or businessman. Or the man who placed a rock on her finger.

Glowing, she would call out to all her friends and family that she was engaged. And she would be the Belle of the Ball for that one day. A day all to herself.

Yes, yes. Her day. "Me. And my mother's."

And even though that woman is not the one you ever thought you could identify with, somewhere in that dream there is also a tiny piece of you. Maybe it's the dress. Maybe it's a ring. Maybe it's the fact that he gets down on his knee. Maybe it's his promise to take the hair out of the shower drain for the rest of your lives.

And occasionally, that part awakens.

It helps, of course, that your partner shares this dream. Or the cultural understanding. As we age, weddings of course mean different things. There are new ideas of look and feel. To bridesmaid or not to bridesmaid. And a lot of the world's princes are already married —maybe to you. But usually to others.

And you wonder, or maybe you don't, *Will it be me? Is this me?*

What do we really want? What do these stories really mean?

And then you wonder, *Is this all there is?*

SCRIBBLES
ABOUT
WOMEN

"Life doesn't go in straight lines"

— RUTH SHELL

On Hair

Today I'd like to talk about hair.

Firstly, did everyone out there know that fake eyelashes, and eyelash extensions for that matter, involve human hair?

Well, now you do.

They grow out.

Estimated time: one day to three weeks.

If you are raising an eyebrow at me and feel I'm raising one at you, well, I am.

Only not on purpose. My recent trip to the beautician has left me with one eyebrow permanently raised.

I may be overreacting. Or not. *Yes, yes, I will attempt to pencil it in. If I figure out where to pencil.*

"Don't worry," a friend said.

"They grow out."

Estimated time: one month.

Which brings me to another horrible experience I had three months ago. I have yet to be able to revisit my hairdresser.

I have thought about cheating on him. But he does good hair.

Only last time, after swearing he wouldn't cut it short, he . . .

Well, you know how this story ends.

I may have killed him at the time. Really. It was AMAZING how bad I felt after this.

For two days I felt like shit about myself. My boyfriend told me I was being dumb.

It only stopped when ten people told me how good my hair looked, or at least acknowledged it looked fine. Yes. I am vain.

But more importantly, haircuts have power. And yes, yes.

They grow out.

Estimated time: three to six months. Or one year if it was a real hack job. Sorry.

I read once that Kate Winslet was asked to wear a merkin* for a movie she where was to appear nude in and that was set in the 1930s.

She said, "Look, I can let it grow back, but I draw the line at a merkin."

They grow out.

Estimated time: long enough for her to make the movie.

*Yes, I am deliberately making you look up merkin if you don't know what it is. Your whole life will be changed. Or you will chuckle.

49 Things I've Learned

1. I am not skinny from birth and thus will have to work for the body I have more and more as I get older. And I may have to eat less.

2. I do not look particularly good in fluorescent colors, horizontal stripes . . . I do OK in polka dots.

3. Short and tight are very objective terms.

4. I am able to go shorter than I used to.

5. I will never ever look like Elle Macpherson, Helena Christensen, Kate Moss . . . or Julie who still looks the best of all my high school friends. That said, I also will never have the ass of Kim Kardashian, and I should probably aim toward the likes of Reese Witherspoon—at least she's closer to my height.

6. There are positives to #5. No one will ever write about me in *Us Weekly* or *People Magazine*, and no one out there except my dear friends and family and you cares who I'm with or not with. No one will write nasty things about me one week after saying I'm the best thing in the world.

Nor will I be written up under "Worst bods in Hollywood" and spread over E!

7. I am not attracted to Brad Pitt (I've met him). I can't write the same about Angelina (I've met her, too).

8. Johnny Depp ~~is married. He is single.~~ He is married.

9. Ewan McGregor is married.

10. Being judgmental about tummy tucks, Botox, Restylane, microdermabrasion, boob lifts, liposuction, and so forth all decreases proportionally with age.
Never say never (especially if you've never seen what breastfeeding does to breasts).

11. Sadly, in the nature vs. nurture debate, genes do matter.

12. Yes, I (and you) am turning into our mothers.

13. All people will die. And some you care about are dead already.

14. There will always be someone else.

15. Life can be cruel.

16. But thankfully, it is also kind.

17. I don't need to be eighty and wearing a purple hat to know that the less you care, and more fun you have with it all, the more fun it will be and the less you'll care . . . and the happier you'll be too.

Unfortunately I am still working on connecting that knowledge with day-to-day wardrobe crises.

18. (Most) men age better than women. The good news is, there is still love and recommended improvements in:
personality, income and wisdom to look forward to. And there is also #10.

19. Start yoga now. You'll thank me when you are eighty. I plan on thanking me when I'm eighty.

20. I still suck at relationships.

21. I still don't understand men.

22. I still blush when the coffee guy teases me in the morning and says he's missed me.

23. Lists are incredibly gratifying.

24. If you find yourself suddenly feeling you need to be married, it may be because of you. BUT it is also because of the media.
   And Hollywood. And your mother. And your peers. And your age. And where you live.

25. If you find yourself suddenly feeling broody, it may be because of you. BUT it is also because there is a massive baby boom. And Hollywood. And the global financial crisis. And your mother or a well-meaning person. And your peers. And your age. And where you live. And how recently you've held a newborn. Did I mention it is also because of the media—fuck, *Vogue* just told me the "250,000 eggs I had at 25 have become 50,000 at 30 and . . ." I ripped it up.

26. My best friend was right—she told me when I was fifteen that men didn't need to get married any-more because everyone sleeps with them and lives with them anyway.

27. Love DOES exist.

28. Small things. It's in the small things.

29. Lessons are like mold. They come back again and again until they are dealt with. And sometimes professional help and chemicals are necessary on this path.

30. Some lessons are life lessons. They are for life. (I stole that from a guy named Allan Seale).

31. Sometimes it's very hard to know the difference between twenty-nine and thirty.

32. I am still a grasshopper.

33. "Thank you" and "I'm sorry" are magical words. And "please" isn't bad either.

34. Hugs are even more magical.

35. Love and making love are still magical.

36. Be kind. Especially to yourself.

37. Yes, you will cry. At the most inopportune times. Often when you are angry. And possibly at work.

38. "Be" is a very big two-letter word.

39. Friends rock.

40. Travel rocks.

41. Parents quite suddenly get older.

42. Life doesn't go in straight lines.

43. You have not yet learned the art of making your boyfriend (and people at work) do things that you've come up with while having them think they've come up with it.

44. Smile lines are nicer than frown lines.

45. A can of paint is a quick way to fix most ugly living situations.

46. When you are overwhelmed, start with a corner.

47. When you are stressed: Stop. Breathe.

48. Just breathe.

49. Keep breathing.

Things That Worry Us

Our . . .
Lips too thin
Lips too full
Calves too wide
Cankles
Thighs too large
Hips too wide
Ass too big
Ass too small
Ass too flat
Ass too saggy
Ass dimples
Cellulite
Belly too large
Love handles
Boobs too small
Boobs too large
Boobs too saggy
Nipple size
Nipple color
Eye shape (for various eye-makeup trends)
Eyelashes too short
Eyelashes too light

Eyebrow shape
Eyebrow bald spots
Hair too straight
Hair too curly
Hair too thin
Hair too short
Hair too mousy
Body too tall
Body too skinny
Body too fat
Nose too big
Nose too long
Nose too crooked
Nose too bumped
Nose too freckled
Freckles, wherever they are
Eye sight too near / far (glasses / contacts)
Hands too large
Fingers too stumpy
Nails too bitten or short
Strange toes
Feet too large
Feet too ugly
Ears too large
Belly button too outy
That pimple that appeared overnight
That mole
That wrinkle between our brows. Or forehead. Or
neck. Or . . . wrinkles
Chin dimples . . .

Honestly, it's amazing we ever go outside.

And because I refuse to leave us depressed: Just remember you can't have all of these at once. You are not alone. And probably look MUCH better than you think. Now leave that mirror alone and go have some fun. And remember, most boys (or gals if that's your thing) just want us naked.

Things People Don't Talk About

Things People Don't Tell You About or "Forget" to Mention—In No Specific Hierarchy

- Not to use fabric softener on towels
- Abortion
- Female facial hair (unless you live in the Middle East or in the Mediterranean, in which case they may casually remind you that it's time to attend to your moustache over a business lunch)
- How much they actually earn
- How much they actually paid for their apartment
- Depression (Normal. You are not alone . . . there is help.)
- That most engagement stories are not romantic. At least not the lead up. The end bit may / may not be
- That our words have a big impact on what kind of life we live
- Female nipple hair
- Mice, rats, and other vermin who have decided to take up residence in our houses (apparently ants and cockroaches are acceptable topics to broach)

- That women still earn a LOT less than men doing the same jobs
- Who they voted for (in a room of people who display the opposite views)
- How much sex they're really having
- That they are actually judgmental assholes
- That when you are talking about your problems they are thinking, *Thank God that isn't me! / How does this relate to me? / Could this happen to me?*
- How much *Law & Order* they really watch
- Whether they've had chlamydia (rampant in all cities)
- That reading gossipy magazines with stories like "stars without their makeup" makes them feel better about themselves
- How they bought their house (bank of ma & pa, inheritance, lottery . . .)
- How amazing they / their partner is in bed (until they break up)
- The faces / sounds they make when they orgasm
- How long it took them to get pregnant (if it wasn't really, really fast or really, really long)
- How long they have sex for
- How often they orgasm, on average
- How many people they've slept with
- That they feel alone / lonely (nothing to be ashamed of)
- That affairs are really common (which doesn't make it wrong / right. Just common, like divorce)

- That 9–5 type business hours are a relic of some past idea (the factory) and have little to do with how we actually work . . . (like train tracks, which measure the width of a chariot)
- We are constantly over- and underestimating the influence of our environment on us (our moods, our behaviors . . . our everything)
- That it's easier to disagree with and identify why you don't like someone's lifestyle choices rather than confront your own choices
- Abuse (domestic, emotional, physical)
- How much time we spend on our phones / computers
- We are (often) really hard on ourselves
- That everyone we meet is a mirror
- Big brother IS watching. And we are helping him
- How many people read astrologyzone.com
- Trust your intuition. (I know people actually tell you to do this—but then they question you when you do it . . . Trust yourself.)
- Most of us really just want the world to agree with us (and have a short fuse when it doesn't)
- Like REALLY want the world to agree with us
- It will happen. The universe just doesn't tell time like we do.
- Rape
- Masturbation

On Lines & Things

"I swear my wrinkles appeared the day I turned thirty-one."

"Not thirty?"

"No. Maybe that's why I thought thirty was so good? I thought, *Gee, they lied.* Only they didn't, they just meant your thirties."

"Well, my ass has dropped."

"It has not! . . . And the worst part is, I looked back at photos and they were there before . . .only now they are kind of permanent."

"I'm sure all the worrying isn't helping."

"It definitely isn't! I've become crazy . . . I'll catch myself staring at little kids' faces and seeing their pure sweet unlined skin and telling my skin, *Hey, remember how to be like that!*"

Hahahah, "You're a riot."

"Seriously though, do we need to show the passage of time? This is a question that has been plaguing me lately."

"As opposed to world peace?"

"Tell me you've never thought about your neck. Or your eyes . . . or whatever."

"OK, fine, I have thought about all of these, that's why I use rose hip oil and try to get eight hours sleep and have regular facials."

"You do not!"

"Well I intend to!"

"Fine. And we all know how we both don't act all judgmental with Botox anymore."

"Yes, but it's a slippery slope . . ."

"My best friend calls it a tax on aging."

"The main problem is you can't go back. For ten years at least . . . and then . . . if you keep doing it you end up being convinced you need chin and cheek implants . . . and one day you'll wake up one of those weird-cat-eye-raised-eye-browed-waxy-smooth-faced-ladies . . ."

"At least I started with cat eyes."

"Shut up. . . . I was watching some awards show last night. And it made me deeply concerned. Only I was trying hard not to be so I wouldn't frown."

"This red carpet thing . . . it's all the same people as last year, and they look the same. All of them, without a single wrinkle. And this is NOT because of plant-based / crazy diets / detox and healthy life-style, whatever they say."

"No, it's the loving hands of doctors, makeup artists and cosmetic dermatologists."

"Fine, we all know this, but it makes me question— in a way that keeps my face as still and frown-free as possible—what are we meant to look like?"

The {Celebrity} Secret

Have you noticed every time someone asks a celebrity who is looking gorgeous, thin, and unlined:
"What's your secret?"

Their answer is: "I do everything you're meant to do: I eat right, I sleep, I exercise, I'm happy . . ."

What they really mean, if they're not under twenty-two, is:

- I have a great chef. Or, I don't actually eat much. Or both. I also drink a lot of water.
- I have a great personal trainer and exercise six times a week for two hours at a time.
- *Not three to four times for forty minutes.*
- I have a great facialist, makeup artist, hairdresser, dermatologist, cosmetic dermatologist, and likely, plastic surgeon.
- I may or may not use Botox.
- But there are other things like Fraxal, skin peels, microdermabrasion . . . and a makeup artist to cover anything up that's still not "perfect" or "smooth."

- I have a personal assistant, manager, and lots of people to do all that annoying stuff that stresses me out.
- I sleep and I'm happy.

Which may or may not be true, but I certainly don't have a problem lying about them either way.

''I didn't know what
I wanted to do. But I
knew the woman
I wanted to be.''

— DIANE VON FURSTENBERG

DATING

What is the goal of dating?

". . . so write her
a check"

"She's not interested
in money; she's
interested in love"

"I thought that line
was discontinued"

— THE MOVIE *SABRINA*

Love Potion

A friend once sent me an article from the *New York Times*. And it moved me. And made me cry. Just a little. A woman who visits a rabbi out of desperation looking for a blessing to marry gets just that. The rabbi releases a curse. And says there will be a man by Hanukkah. "Sagur." "Closed." Done deal.

It reminded me of my visit to my wax lady last week who told me she visited a rabbi in her early twenties when she was stressed about life, not being married. *In my head I immediately revised early twenties to late twenties / early thirties on account of my own age and those of us in my generation.*

What he told her was, in essence, that she would be married, have kids. But more importantly, that she would do something, heal, with her hands. Having gone to her for the last six months and having very limited hair re-growth and enjoying her energy very much I can only say, marriage predictions aside, he was dead-on about her hands.

So the idea of visiting a rabbi has snuck up twice in one week. Three times if I add the wise African man who told a friend waht her next calling would be— which was so removed from her current job that she appropriately laughed—only to find herself doing exactly as told some two years down the track.

A rabbi in these stories is nothing if not a wise man, a teacher, a healer all rolled into one.

There is a concept in Hassidic literature, by rabbis, that if you tell the right person the right story at the right time, you can change the world. Every person being a world. The world easily changed in the space between words. Things open and shift.

As a storyteller, I have heard and know of this concept. The story that wills to be spoken. Even when it is not at all the one you have prepared. Like this one. And I too have been waiting for my world to be changed by a woman or man who tells me what is next. Who gives my future an anchor toward which to shift. A fulcrum and lever from my fears. And at the same time I have shunned it. Run away from it. Refused it as it came up. For precisely the same reason. I believe and know that words and stories can act as such a shift. I know how badly I wish to grasp at what's next. To know it and bring it into existence exactly as foretold. I am also, like perhaps many of my generation, scared. Scared of the options it removes, as much as the security it provides. Were I to be given the choice, I would choose freedom over chains. And wind in my sails over a large home with a garden.

I also know that you don't need to visit another. That you can do it for yourself. Change your own world. And your own story. If there is a God in all of us, then there is a God in me, too. I don't know much about the predictions of rabbis or psychics, or letting predictions come true. I have avoided them. And that. But I do know about the power of the woman who sits next to you on the bus and turns to you and says "It will be OK." Or your grandmother who reminds you that life doesn't go in straight lines and that you wouldn't want it to. And I am also wondering, right now, whether a visit to a rabbi might be necessary. And as such am saying OK. If it comes up again I will try it. Why refuse the hold of a friendly hand that is offered? Why does it always have to come from yourself?

Did You Know?

". . . there hasn't been a single innovation in birth control for men in the last four hundred years?"

Round of giggles.

We're drinking again. This time at my best friend's apartment. Whom I've noticed isn't drinking much. Hmmm.

"Think about it. It's great that in the 1800s they wanted to put birth control in the hands of women. And accessibility of condoms is really cool—except in countries where religion and the Pope tried to block it—so no innovation. None. Drug companies are more concerned with finding the next Viagra than a male pill."

"But would you really trust a guy to take a pill daily?" another friend asks.

"I don't care . . . the pill wreaks havoc with my hormones. My skin sucks, I get fat, and depressed . . . and I also don't get those names like Brenda, Yasmin . . ."

"I'm on Diana," my best friend cuts in.

"And it's because whoever makes them is a guy,

and it's the only thing he can offer his partner—a pill named after her."

More giggles.

"OK, that's pretty funny," I concede.

"But aren't we meant to be modern and share in these responsibilities and freedoms?"

"Maybe we're not as modern as we think," my best friend says, straightening up.

"In psychology there was this psychologist named David Buss. Sounded like a bit of an asshole, really. Only a rather clever one.

"He had some theory about how we haven't really evolved beyond men sowing their oats and women looking for a stable partner who could provide for her and her offspring. Because if not, then women would sleep around as much as men because they had control—birth control and condoms—to prevent them from being harmed by the process . . ."

"What??"' all four of us shout in unison.

"Oh, it got worse, this is the part I remember, my (female) lecturer implied he used it as a way to pick up students / women."

"How?"

"Whenever they argued with him he'd say, OK, how about we go out back and, you know . . . if you think that would be fun . . ."

"Well, you've got to give it to him. He certainly got more than tenure out of that."

"That's really interesting, but where does that leave me? I've gone off the pill, but if I hear one more guy say 'but we don't really need a condom, I'm clean,' I might scream. . . ."

"Maybe you can invent something?" one of the girls suggests.

"Oh, I already have."

"What is it?"

"Can't say, it's proprietary, but I'm pretty sure it will be big in Japan."

More giggles.

"I need food" one of the girls announced.

"Nutella on toast or Pringles?"

"Both."

. . .

What can I say? We are easily distracted.

It Doesn't (Always) Need to be Complicated

"I'm granting alter-egos. Who do you want to be?" I ask my best friend as I stab at the salad we're sharing.

We're at our local café and the waitress didn't even bother to give us menus.

Just smiled, asked if we wanted their signature salad, no-onion-egg-salad-on-rye for her, roast beef or quiche for me. And did we want our tea iced or hot?

You would think there were no eating options. Truth be told the place has a huge menu.

And we work on a restaurant street. But if we get to go to lunch, we go there.

It looks like a place for women. Which makes it an easy way to avoid eating with my friend's predominantly male team.

But I digress.

"Alter-ego? I think I'll be pregnant."

"Really?" That was unexpected. She is single, high profile, and manages a huge team of mostly geeky, socially inept men . . . but what the hell?

"OK, with a guy you're with, or by a happy accident, or you don't know which of two guys?" I play along.

Slight frown.

"I think a great guy I love."

"Hmmm . . . fine, what's he like?"

"Oh, he's great . . . really nice, nice eyes, but of course, not too nice . . . because there always has to be a drama. . . ."

And as she starts to dream up dramas I interrupt and say, "Do you mind if there aren't any dramas? I mean, why can't there be one of us who is just pregnant, in love with a man who loves her back, and happy?"

She smiles. I mean really smiles. And our profiteroles haven't arrived yet.

(We really go here for the desserts.)

"No drama. Pregnant, in love, and no drama," she repeats. She's got that dreamy look. Which is fine because I just spied our dessert en route. Maybe I can sneak a few extra bites.

Type Theory

What's your type?

Is it the college footballer? The tall guy? The cute little guy who winks at you? The one who makes you laugh till you think you might pee in your pants . . . the one who holds your face when he kisses you . . .

Or some combination?

And what do you expect?

Do you expect him to be the one? One? All? Everything?

Do you want to be rescued? Held? Fixed?

Do you want to be released?

Do you want sex for eight hours?

"Who the hell has sex for eight hours?" one of my girlfriends interrupts my reading.

"Well I did, once, when I was in my early twenties . . ."

"And was it in any way, shape, or form good?"

"Well, um . . . ah . . . Sting and Trudie say they do. And there's Tantra."

"Great, we're believing the junk we read and hear on E! and in magazines again."

My friend chuckles

"Have we taught you nothing?"

"But you've just interrupted me!!!!! I was in the middle of . . ."

"Honey you were in the middle of making every happy gal reading your book of truth suddenly quiver with fear that they should need something like *that* . . .

"Not to mention, who the hell has the time for that after they've orgasmed twice? Don't you guys want to sleep? Personally I'd be bored."

"OK, I hear you" (still a bit miffed at being interrupted).

"That said," my girlfriend adds, "when people say hours, is that the same as having sex two or three times in one night? I mean it happens in a space of like eight hours. I've done *that* tons of times."

"Me too! And I bet so have you." Yes, yes. I had to add that.

We all giggle.

"Fine. I'll concede . . .you're incorrigible. . ." she says shaking her head.

"That's why you love me and let me read to you . . . not to mention that fact that I'm ever so entertaining and lovable."

"Meanwhile, who wants the last piece of tempura?" one of the girls asks.

"You have it."

"Yeah, I might explode."

"I have to say, that's the best thing about this pregnancy thing," she says while pulling up her top slightly, "elasticized waist bands are de rigueur."

"OMG!" (Pronounced OH MY GAWD.) "I forgot about those!!! I had a friend who swore by them. Skinny jeans with elasticized waists."

"I'm thinking they should make them like that for everyone"

"I'd buy them!! Especially for when we go for hamburgers and fries!"

"Mmm, fries. I could go for some fries."

"You just said you were so stuffed you couldn't eat another bite of low-cal sushi."

"But it's FRIES!!!"

More giggles.

"Well, OK, honey, we'll go get fries on the way home—but only if they are the skinny ones. I can't stand the fat ones."

I love my girlfriends.

I really do. *I like the idea of elasticized waistbands for the un-pregnant amongst us too . . . but not as much as I love you all.*

Hope this finds you grinning.

Blessings for sex and cocktails to you.

Horror Stories

Well-intended things people do / say with regards to your singledom:

- You'll regret it. Get on with it.
- Just put yourself out there. Seriously, you have to commit to the idea and date like crazy.
- Insist you go to a fortune teller / numerologist / kabbalist / acupuncturist.
- Have you considered curse removal?
- Offer to bury their firstborn's foreskin and bless it for you.

Dating Horror Stories
I won't bore you with mine. Fill in your own or collect your girlfriends'. Preferably over wine.

"Why do all good kissing scenes happen in the rain?"

— FAR TOO MANY MOVIES TO LIST HERE . . .

Don't Forget to Back Up

My backup is engaged. My ex is married with kids. I'm barely dating. And it has become quite suddenly ridiculously cold at night.

Diaries have been done. Overdone. I think even blog posts have been done since *Julie & Julia*.

I can definitely make this into a small e-book. "Journeys of my Chick Lit" quest. But . . . well.

It's not really there yet.

Oh, there is a bit of good news. Today it's sunny. I'm not at work. And the doc gave my fingers the all-clear. Finally. Bye-bye, bandages! Hello, hands. And in a few weeks, hello, manicure—my Mom would be so proud.

To the Ghosts Who Write History Books

So I went to visit the rabbi.

And then the week disappeared.

New Years is around the corner. My week was long; work was crazy.

And I got kind of sidetracked with various events in life, the universe, and everything.

By the way, this week's title is stolen from a song by The Low Anthem.

I found it via Facebook the other day—posted by one of my random acquaintances—funny they don't have a friendship ranking on Facebook by the way, but perhaps that's a good thing.

I shudder to think what we would all do then!

It's one thing to discover you aren't on your best friend's speed dial.

But quite another to be relegated a friendship grade in public. Multiply that by the four hundred or so "friends" you have (eight hundred if you are under twenty-five, eighty if you're over forty-five– sorry but it's true) and you can imagine how great you'd feel opening your profile.

One can see I'm having a bit of an anti-Facebook stance today.

It could be that I saw three lines on my face in what has to be one of the ugliest photos I've seen of myself, which, even after de-tagging I know must have been seen by at least FORTY of my least loved high school colleagues. . . .

OK so I know I'm almost thirty and they shouldn't matter.

But, let's be honest. One of the benefits of Facebook is stalking.

But only when you are on the looking end and can secretly gloat at how great you look vis-à-vis your least loved high school colleagues.

This long Facebook rant, though true and meant, was just a way to defer what I know very well you all wanted to read and know.

"Um, hello! What did the rabbi say?"

Actually, how many of you scrolled here without reading the above?!

Don't worry. I'd do the same.

Well here's the thing. I used rabbi as a euphemism. I actually went to see a tea lady.

One who reads your stars in your tea leaves.

"OK fine, what did she say?

"And do you have to drag it out?!"

She said some interesting things. Things to mull over. She read me (or the tea) well.

And yes, I'm not quite ready to write about it.

I'll get there. . .

The Quickest Diet Secret

"I've had a genius idea!"

"Uhuh . . . What?"

"We have to go wedding-dress shopping."

"Huh? What?

"Sorry to state the obvious but, um, we're not getting married."

"I know we're not getting married—yet—but . . ."

"OK so trying on dresses will manifest weddings—I've heard it before, genius."

". . . Stop interrupting me!

"I'm sure it can manifest them but that's not the point!

"The point is—it's the best weight-loss gig in town, pop on a white dress and bang! Pounds drop.

"Nothing like seeing your ass or stomach in white."

"OK it's not bad. . . . I'll grant it's novel. . . ."

"Let's go try on some Vera Wang . . ."
"Oh I'm going Marchesa."

"Really? I always imagined you in Prada or something . . ."

And we end our day with . . .

Chocolate cake, naturally.

Optimism for Those without Antibodies

If you're kinda done with your own self-hating marriage trek:

a. You will be married (if you want it).

b. And have a wedding / celebration that makes sense to you and your partner in crime.

c. Accept that it's kinda OK to want things other people want, too. Assuming you've done the work on why and even if the answers are vague, understand that it's coming from you, too.

d. Acknowledging society, subconscious and conscious pressures from the place you live in and the weddings that surround you have probably sped up your marriage yearning processes, and that's OK, too, because it's where you're at.

e. Knowing that it will happen. And if this sounds terrible to write, well I'll just come out and say it, e part 2. knowing that if it's not with him it will be with someone else. Because Ladies, there is always someone else. At least seven someone elses.

What can I say? At heart I'm an optimist.

OK I'm taking my OPI "No Room for the Blues" toes to work.

Have a brilliant day.

Engagement Chicken Recipe

"If really desperate there's a recipe called Engagement Chicken. Yes, really."

Google it.

Sense of Smell

Flies on a carrion:
When a man finds another woman attractive, other men know without knowing they know, and are drawn to her.

So I ended it.
And who do I get an SMS from like less than half an hour later?

My ex from last fall!

I swear it's like they smell it!

SEX

Required Reading

Everything you need to know about sex has already been written.

To catch yourself up try:
The Tantra. Gloria. Nora. Carrie. Lena.

ENGAGEMENT

"My Boyfriend Won't Marry Me"

Prince William Waited

Prince William and Kate Middleton's Engagement Press Conference

1:30 *"So Prince William, why did it take you so long to propose. . .?"*

(It's not just you.)

(Sometimes, it's also the universe telling you something. Only you know the answer.)

I Found My Ring

I found my ring.
 Citrine.

My best friend told me to find a ring.
 A nice chunk or interesting stone of citrine.
 Or a yellow diamond.
 Citrine chunk.
 Yellow.
 Happy yellow, interesting stone.
 Slim band.

Some of us have an idea or know exactly what our ring will look like way before we get engaged or even find a partner.

Some of us have never considered this and find ourselves engaged, with a ring we would never have imagined (and briefly wonder "Does he know me at all?")

Others still will casually save images of rings (what is Pinterest for?) letting their girlfriends / sisters know what they want for when the time comes.

Some clever men propose and suggest you design it together. Others share heirlooms. Others fold a paperclip.

Which are you? What will your story be?

"Everyone else was getting married, and my boyfriend didn't want to buy a couch together."

What Do We Really Want?

A friend turns to me and says "It's not fair . . . I can't deal with it anymore, I get told about weddings and I want to cry . . . and my mom . . . don't even get my started on my mom asking me when I'm getting married. I'm only twenty-eight. . . . What does everyone want from me?"

I don't know . . . and I didn't know what to tell her . . .

Here I am, wondering the same thing (and wondering what I want from myself).

What happened to ME!? I am an optimistic person. I am always so happy for other people and now I hear about weddings and babies and I get a bit . . . I don't know . . . happy for them, but sad for me.

Is this an age thing? A stage thing?

"It will pass," my girlfriends tell me . . .

Fine, I think.

But I want to know why there is so much of it now.

What do I really want from marriage and why has marriage suddenly become a thing for me when all the people who I think are cool are the ones who were pregnant before or did things in their own time in their own way?

I also notice I like to get what I want . . . and more.

I'm just ready.

Something just made me ready . . . to get married.

But I want a happy party.
And I want to dance.

"What can you give up on?"

It's like I keep pushing myself over and over to break something with him and then I think:

Why do we do this?

Why don't we just accept what we have?

Don't underestimate the power of the environment.

If you suddenly want to get married, it may be you.

But it is also society. Listen, if *Vogue* has articles about rings and egg count, it's safe to say it's not just you.

Apropos

I breathe deeply into the phone in case I burst into tears right then and there.

"What, honey?" my girlfriend asks on the other end. "Wait are you OK?"

"I . . . I'm engaged. . . !"

"Oh, wow! That's awesome news—yayayay!!!!!"
  "So he finally got the message?"
  "Um," I sniffled
  "Not exactly."
  And I start to cry
  "Are these not tears of happiness?"
  "Well, yes, but . . ."
  "But . . .?"
  "He didn't ask me."
  "I asked him, and he said yes."
  "Oh," slight pause but my girlfriend quickly catches her breath. "But that's really cool. . . . You were getting frustrated that it wasn't in your control —really, really cool of you. So how did you do it?'"

"Um, yeah . . . that," I said after taking a big nose blow. "I think I'm going to have to make him ask me or take it back," I continued.

"What, Why???"

"Um, well, I was so frustrated and when I heard him come home I kinda just blurted it out and he said 'yes.'"

"See, that's cool!!" she said.

"Um, I was on the toilet!

"I didn't even see his face!"

". . . It's not that bad."

"Yes, yes it is. . . . And I just heard you suck your breath in! And you love me!"

"I carried a watermelon" . . . otherwise known as "I'm getting married!"

I'm Getting Married

So yes. I had intended to start this chick-lit-modern-fairytale-stuff with a digression on my love for Patrick Swayze and *Dirty Dancing*.

After all, who hasn't had an idiot line like "I carried a watermelon" slip out of their mouths in front of some man they are trying to impress. . . .

But let's be honest, that is NOT the story you want to hear!

The subject line, by the way, the "I'm getting married" title was born out of a chat conversation I had with a girlfriend while we were both at work and separated by a twenty hour plane ride so we take whatever modes of communication we can get.

"Hi, how are you?" [insert my response and a few taps of lalala and emoticons] . . .

"I'm getting married!!!!"

At which point I did what we all do—I jumped up and down screamed out loud and picked up my phone because well, fuck work in a situation like this.

Girlfriends are your blood! And this one was getting MARRIED!!"

So yes, she is now married and I am getting married. (Jump up and down—go on, you KNOW you want to . . . or at least use it as an excuse to peruse wedding blogs. As if you have never done that before.)

My partner in crime suddenly decided, just when I had given up and let it go (well, a bit), that now was the right time to get engaged.

And it turns out that while I don't feel different (except now I do have a good excuse to peruse said blogs) and we don't feel any different, I am every bit aglow from the fact that he understood the importance of "the romantic gesture" to me.

All of which is me waxing philosophical—but I don't want to turn this into a fairy tale or even chick lit. That would be both untrue and not, well . . . not as beautiful as real life for me.

They lied to us. Again. Engagement does not exist. It is simply a euphemism for "When are you getting married?"

If you're getting married, trust me, you'll need this answer:

The answer is, *"Thank you, we're really happy being engaged right now! We'll let you know as soon as we set the date."*

(You'll soon find out that all anyone cares about is rushing you to the next stage . . . perhaps to confirm that his or her path is the right one . . .)

The Wedding Collection

Otherwise known as "I'm getting married!!!"

Which really should be "we're getting married," but by now you know, if not personally then from experience, that that's simply not how it works.

Actually it could also be known as "my wedding," or, to quote one bride-to-be, "mine, and my mother's." But I digress, and you haven't even gotten past the title yet.

In my short span of engaged life, I have learned many lessons for the modern bride.

Here they are:

1. Hold onto the moment you are engaged. It will soon be turned into . . . "when are you getting married?" Which is to say, "engaged" is a fake concept. They lied to us. Again. Sorry.

And I really don't understand why I still fall for this stuff!

2. It turns out I really just wanted to be engaged (more on this in a bit). Or rather, I just wanted to be asked. And he asked very nicely. In Paris.

3. Weddings stress me out a little. Even a lot. Perhaps because they involve family, other people's families, realizing you have a lot of family you will have to invite, and mostly because I have a lot of ideas and tend to want things to be perfect. Only now I am thirty, so I can also add I know nothing is perfect (and that's good) and that it will always involve family and I want it to be simple but simple my way is often a lot of work. And maybe I like to make things complicated and don't let go enough. Maybe.

4. I will try to keep bridesmaids out of it.

5. I *would* make a fabulous bridezilla if current inspiration-wedding-blog-bookmark-pile is any indication (have thus far resisted tumblr'ing/ Pinterest'ing but . . . maybe not for long).

6. I like to be self-righteous and pretend to know that the wedding is not a marriage and is not where most of your energy should go.

7. Party favors are not even a traditional concept, yet I find them awfully cute.

8. There will be no bridesmaids. Sorry. I do love my girlfriends, but you will have to find your own dresses. You may have to zip my dress up in a photo though.

9. Sorry. I also love wedding albums, good photographers, and photo booths. Prepare yourselves.

10. Thankfully, due to family commitments, it will be next year. Ooh. My first Save the Date. On this note, does anyone know the etiquette on sending Save the Dates? I know you do.

11. Yes, however intimate the idea may be, it will get bigger by the minute. Unless you elope. If you have a family who won't mind and it speaks to you, I suggest this option. Take a photographer though.

12. I will be a mini-mini-bridezilla, and I'll have a FABULOUS dress and shoes.

13. Outsource as much as you can.

14. I really think, in hindsight, the best way to get married is to get pregnant and just have to get married before you show too much. If you care about that. Or wait until baby can make an adorable flower girl. Or whatever. You know, the chill way. Those weddings were always fabulous.

Phew, now that that's sorted, where were we? It's hard to know with the whirlwind.

Here is a snippet:
"I'm getting married!!!!!!"
" . . ."
"Are you there?"
"Ah, yes, I just wanted to make sure you weren't gonna cry . . ."
"Oh, (little chuckle), no, no *he asked me.* Like, for real, with a ring and everything!"
"And do you like it?"
[*Long pause*]

"I don't not like it. . ."

"Phew, guess what honey? You're just like everyone else!"

"Really?"

"Sure, unless you literally went with him, which by the way lots of people think is the right thing to do, however unromantic. . .most girls freak out a bit about their rings. But then it grows on you, and you love the sentiment."

"Oh, I love you. . ."

"Oh honey, I love you too. . .now, how did he propose. . .?"

"Well, I was meant to be heading to that work conference I told you about, you know where we could bring partners to the event and. . ."

PS

I have already freaked out twice - not about my guy, no that's all good. First, about something too silly to mention. But it involved a tantrum. Mine. Oh Lord, teach me how to let go! And second, on what the hell design do we need for Save The Dates? Which I don't actually even care about!

''There's very little
that can't be fixed
with strawberries
and cream.
Or a bath.''

THE WEDDING

ADVICE
(FOR WANT OF A BETTER WORD):

"Don't worry sweetheart, I promise it'll all be fine. Try not to have a picture in your head beforehand of how it 'should' be."

Last Name

"So, are you changing your name?"

It occurred to me recently that I was perplexed by how many women I know are still changing their names. Rather, it perplexed me more that it was assumed they would. How many post-wedding Facebook comments congratulate Mr. & Mrs. X, without asking if she has changed hers but, rather, assuming she has. To his.

As such, I have conducted a totally unscientific study, and these are my results, in order of common-ality, not importance.

I. Reasons of Age:

Under twenty-nine—chances of changing your name are higher, mostly because who you are is less established vis-à-vis in your career and life.

Twenty-nine to thirty—borderline years. I can't say why. But it just seems as such, on the balance, that your chances of changing your name are higher than below twenty-eight, but lower than above thirty.

Over thirty—chances of changing your name are thus lower, for same reasons as above. You've been you for longer.

II. Reasons of Importance
It's important to him. / It's important to his family. / It's important to the family. (Yes, usually his).

III. Reasons of Vanity & Ego:
You have a surname you simply don't care for. (I have a gorgeous girlfriend whose name was Harlot.)

You have a distinct first name, making your surname redundant. (I have a gorgeous friend named Cressida.)

IV. Reasons called "Feminist:"
You simply don't understand why the hell you should.

But there are a whole lot of people who will snarl and bark "feminist" in such a way as to imply it is both a dirty word and they think you should, too.

V. Reasons of Background:
You are from any of these backgrounds: Russian, Spanish, South American . . .

The idea is similar in assumption, but the outcome slightly different—whereby instead of specifically taking HIS name, you will take a mother's surname, or, everyone's surnames, for five generations.

VI. Reasons of Union:

This plays out in several ways:

i. Whereby you can't decide and decide to create your own one. Sometimes a hybrid. Sometimes for the sound. (Currently trending in Israel.)

ii. Whereby you decide any products of the union, aka children, must have the same surname (his or both, rarely yours).

iii. Whereby you join both names. (Popular in Europe. Though the hyphen is losing its charm.)

VII. Reasons of Immigration:

You need a Visa, Green Card, etc.

VIII. Reasons of status:

Whereby you are marrying a prince or someone titled and it simply "wouldn't do."

IX. Reasons of "Blank Stare"

i. Whereby you explain to me you have no intentions of getting married. Ever.

ii. Whereby you can't understand the question.

On Bridesmaids

Bridesmaids I
An ensemble of four (or three or seven or . . .) and the various thoughts different girls have once they become brides-to-be/bridesmaids:

Every wedding needs bridesmaids, don't you think?

Bridesmaids, I hated being a bridesmaid.
   I loved being a bridesmaid.
   The dress. [*Snigger*[
   The dress!!!! [*Happy sigh*]
   Those dresses. [*Happy*]
   Those dresses! [*Horrified*]
   Why would you put four women in the same dress?
   Why?
   Why?
   I just don't get it.
   I totally get why.

It's tradition.

It ties the wedding together.

It ties the wedding together.

It's amazing how it ties the wedding together. Especially in photos.

The photos.

I hate those posed photos.

It really ties the color palette together.

Pink.

Pinks.

Everyone looks good in pink.

You can all come in whatever dress you want. As long as it's pink.

If only it was a bit tighter and had less ribbons. And was less, well, pink.

Why do they have to wear pink? No one looks good in hot pink. No one.

I went with silver. I couldn't bear to see any more shades of pink.

A rainbow of pastels. That way they could all look good. Although no one wanted to be peach.

They drew straws for that.

You should all have the same hair, and shoes.

Not too matchy-matchy. Similar is good. I drew the line at the same nail polish. Though I did encourage fake tan.

I wanted my bridesmaids to look amazing, so I told them to wear whatever they wanted.

I wanted my bridesmaids to feel comfortable. So I let them choose the style and their hair. But we went shopping for the same shoes.

I wanted to wear my hair down. So I asked them to all have up-dos.

Consistency is important.
Hem lines are important.
Above the knee is so uncouth.
Gently flowing below the knee.
Long. Their dresses have to be long.
Everyone looks good in a bustier and long skirt.
Everyone looks good in strapless.
Everyone looks good in A-line.

When have you seen women willingly choosing to wear the same outfits?
No one looks as good in the same dress as the person standing next to them.
The only thing that everyone looks good in is black.

Black. You can't have black at a wedding.
How can you not have bridesmaids at a wedding? They help you organize the bachelorette party, the bridal shower. They are your people.

Bridesmaids are key.

I didn't want to offend anyone so I had seven.

We had three.

We had four because we had four groomsmen. Symmetry is important.

We had three groomsmen and four bridesmaids. It wasn't a problem, one just had to walk in alone.

I had none. And my girlfriends threw me a shower. They were awesome.

I hated my bachelorette party. They didn't make enough of an effort. I mean, I'm the bride. I should be the center of attention.

Bridesmaids II
The Cost So Far

$$$ Dress

$$ Shoes

$$$ Hair and makeup

$$ Gift for wedding

$ Gift for bridal shower

$$ Bridal shower cost per bridesmaid

$$ Bachelorette party dinner, drinks, stripper, etc. per person attending

$$ Bachelorette party accessories per bridesmaid (fake penises, chocolate penises, cupcakes, etc.)

Wedding Brain

OK, if you got to our age, you've probably heard of Pregnancy Brain. Or Baby Brain.

How your brain becomes stupid and forgetful toward the end of pregnancy, and during the first year of your kids' entrance into the world. Well, it's a known and quite heavily researched topic.

Today I want to talk about a far less researched behavior. I'm calling it "Wedding Brain." Wedding Brain is not the part of you that turns into a psychopath or bridezilla. Wedding Brain is the part of you who is quite suddenly NOT able to concentrate on work. Its superpower has not yet been discovered, but certain musical interludes that would previously have been written off as sappy suddenly pull at the heartstrings. When under its influence, a bride-to-be can sit for quite a few minutes smiling contently, just knowing her wedding is soon, and she can talk endlessly about the wedding.

My brain feels like it's gone fishing. Except when it comes to pom-poms. Or wedding blogs. We need research. Well-defined social psychology studies that document this phenomenon.

Or, you can just come over and watch me puttering about with a stupid smile on my face.

Whatever works.

Perspective

A note on hotel weddings, and weddings in general.

It never occurred to me until recently, because of my other work, why I hadn't been particularly bothered by certain details of our wedding, like centerpieces, tablecloth patterns, flower and candle height, and other such important measures. These things ARE important (the devil is in the details, the details make the design, and all that) but they are rendered all the more important when one is getting married in a hotel / conference center room.

Because those rooms are in general. UGLY AS FUCK.

I mean no disrespect. Really I don't.

But if you've ever seen those rooms with the lights on you'll notice two things:

1. REALLY REALLY ugly patterned carpet (designed to hide all manner of stains and keep the noise inside the room).

2. EQUALLY REALLY REALLY ugly curtains.

If this is the room that you now need to transform to a magical wedding scene then all manner of details become key.

Most importantly to DISTRACT ones eye from such ugliness.

If you are getting married outside at, say, a vineyard, these details become less important.

I repeat.

(Almost) no one has ever walked out of a wedding and said, "You know, those tablecloths really let the wedding down."

Perspective, people.

(Though I really hear you on distracting from that carpet. High flowers and mood lighting is going to be high on your budget.)

"This is not the
time to sort out
your relationship
with your mother /
mother-in-law.
There are other
times.
This is not it."

101 Sources of {Wedding} Stress

- Your period is due the weekend of the wedding.
- You are fighting with your fiancé on a regular basis.
- Your mother is killing you softly.
- Your friend has offered to make invitations, and you can't say no.
- Your mother hates the invitations, and you now have to get new ones made.
- It is less than (two*) months to the wedding, and you still haven't (found a photographer*) [*insert relevant time frame and important thing you haven't done].
- Everyone assures you two hundred fifty people is fine, even if your hall has a maximum capacity of one hundred fifty.
- Two hundred fifty people have said they are coming and your hall has a maximum capacity of one hundred fifty.
- Your period is still due the weekend of the wedding.
- Your fiancé doesn't want to talk about it.
- You don't want to talk about it.

- Flower girls dresses cost almost the same as yours.
- Jimmy Choos don't ship to where you live.
- Sudden excitement over bakers twine.
- The photographer cancelled.
- The DJ cancelled.
- The DJ insists on leaving the song list up to his / her discretion.
- Your bridesmaids love what you have asked them to wear. *Lies. Either they are lying to you because they are too polite, they are all identical sizes, or you are letting them choose what to wear.*
- You realize hot pink does not look good on everyone.
- Your bridesmaids are not being understanding. *My only recommendation for this is to remember when you've been a bridesmaid.*
- Everyone keeps telling you how soon the wedding is. *Do they think you don't know?*
- Your mother-in-law isn't speaking to you.
- Your mother is speaking to you. Often.
- You've realized it isn't your wedding. It's (insert name of offending family members or parties).
- You see a photo on Facebook and your arms look much fatter than your remembered.
- People keep telling you how much they enjoyed planning their wedding. *Most people lie or have bad memories.*
- It's two months to go and you forgot to . . . (etsy.com or forget about it).
- DIY takes a lot longer than expected especially if crafty is not your thing.
- Number of guests who RSVP'd . . . or didn't.

- The weather forecast on your wedding day: sunny with a gentle breeze.
- You don't have a wedding planner.
- You have a wedding planner.
- You are over budget.
- You are way over budget.
- What budget?
- Your fiancé suggests eloping.
- You want to kill your fiancé (and thus wonder why you want to marry him?).
- Your fiancé is incredibly understanding about everything and has been pleasantly involved and only opinionated in the best possible way. *Just checking that you are reading. This is a LIE. This does not happen . . . even the nicest of guys have been known to break. And if you have one who hasn't— congratulations! You are the exception. Or you are a fabulous liar.*
- How the hell can invitations cost so much?
- How many grams is paper meant to be?
- Printed addresses on envelopes are suddenly unacceptable. *People have been known to hold up envelopes to see if they are real calligraphy ink. I only know two antidotes for this: 1. Don't care what other people think 2. Let whichever family member cares pay.*
- Your parents are "helping" you pay for the wedding. *I have no problem with this, but if you have some money saved, my recommendation is back away slowly and surely.*
- You just realized again this is not your wedding. It isn't. The good news is, it *is* a celebration of you and your partner.

- Favors. They seem to be everywhere. What the hell is a wedding favor? And why do you need one? *No idea, but apparently some people think you do. Do what you think. And if you can't, well . . . etsy.com, nice tea, candy or a fortune cookie. No one needs some tchotchke with your name on it. Really, they don't.*
- The wedding list.
- The forty-five friends your (insert name of offender/s) needs to invite whom he / she last saw in kindergarten.
- How do you incorporate people you work with into your ever expanding wedding list?
- You REALLY need to eat carbs and chocolate. Often. But you also REALLY want to fit into your wedding dress. *My only suggestion here is to go for a walk while you eat chocolate and carbs. Or, like with most things, try and keep your mouth shut.*
- (If you are going to a dressmaker, do not read this.) You had your wedding dress made, and you hate it. It looks nothing like it was meant to. *I promise this happens to a lot of people. People just don't tell you they bought two dresses. And they don't like to admit they were wrong. Go buy another dress if you need to. I give you permission.*
- Your wedding invitation is not a representation of you as a couple.
- Branding your wedding. *You are not a brand.*
- You have turned into a psychopath. And you don't know what to do.
- People who tell you that during their wedding

planning they were not stressed. Amnesia and lies. Ignore them.

- You wake up in a cold sweat thinking about seating arrangements.
- You wake up in a cold sweat thinking about wedding favors.
- You don't like the tablecloths. *Please remind self when was the last time you walked out of a wedding and said, "Wow, the tablecloths really let me down."*
- You know you have turned into bridezilla but you can't help it. You just want it to be perfect.
- The wedding list keeps expanding. Who are these people??
- Your fiancé has asked you (kindly/unkindly) to please NOT talk about the wedding.
- Your perfectly folded origami cranes that were strung across trees have been rained on.
- You are seriously shit at DIY.
- You may have to fire your wedding planner.
- You fired your wedding planner.
- You hate your invitations.
- Your partner thinks he is doing someone a favor by NOT inviting them. ("Who likes weddings?")
- You just had your hair trial.
- You just had your makeup trial. Drag queens wear less.
- You went to a wedding and they had a LOT of the same ideas as you.
- You have not miraculously lost [X] pounds.
- Wedding blogs. Stop looking at them.
- I said stop!

A few sources of wedding joy and laughter:

- Bridal magazine and blogs (because I know you're reading them).
- Your fiancé reminding you that it's "just invitations/confetti/tablecloths" (but only when timed appropriately and intoned correctly or else it may end up on the other list).
- Your girlfriends.
- Your decision not to have bridesmaids.
- Feeling very loved.
- Finally learning the answer to "do you want me to help?" and "how can I help?" ("Yes," and "Please help us make one thousand origami cranes").
- Remembering it's just a wedding. It's just a wedding.
- The little book: *Scenes from an Impending Marriage* by Adrian Tomine.
- You have a photo booth (they are really easy to set up if you don't have one yet).
- People at work are suddenly very understanding when you get really mad about something.
- You realize you love your partner even when he annoys you.
- The day (*I'm assured of this*) is awesome.
- Weddings are magical. Yes, even the biggest cynic (me) knows this.
- Fake eyelashes are awesome.

To Read on the Week of Your Wedding

Things I've learned this week so far (four days to go):

- This is not your wedding. (*Yes, I may have mentioned this before but I haven't LEARNED it yet, clearly.*) Or to put it more eloquently, "The marriage is about you, the wedding is not. . . . It's also about your family and friends."
- You will, on occasion act five years old. And may want to throw a tantrum. You can probably resist the latter. On the former, think "watermelon."
- No matter what you do, someone (possibly your mother) will have something to say about how you can: improve it, change it, make it different, explain how actually it's not meant to be that way, and so forth.
- When people say to you, "Maybe you should," what they mean is, "What I would do." If this is your mother/father/family member this means, "What you SHOULD do, because this is what I would do".
- Laugh as much as you can.

- Fathers of the bride get excited and emotional too.
- At this stage, yoga is a state you probably will only achieve during an actual yoga class.
- Your partner looks VERY cute in his wedding outfit.
- You love your partner VERY much.
- If you get mad at each other over something stupid, stop it midway and say, "Sorry, I am stressed. I know it's stupid." Invariably they will say sorry, too.
- I love making lists, but I love crossing things off much, much more!
- DIY is best done with friends. And laughter. And some really tasty snacks.
- You are probably currently at your most theatrical—write some of those stories down (or tell me). You'll never believe they happened afterward.
- You may not miraculously lose weight. Or to quote myself, "If you don't give up food and don't do exercise, you are unlikely to drop pounds." But you will look glowy and great and your dress will fit.
- My friends are simply incredible.
- My family is amazing.
- Parents or other involved parties can be sources of stress. Now that you know it's also their wedding and about them, maybe they won't be.
- You are probably NOT going to solve your problems with family at the wedding. So perhaps the best advice here is tread lightly. And be immensely kind to yourself.

- You do NOT need to be a bridezilla. At least, not as a goal.
- You forgot how much you prefer to be behind the camera than in front of it.
- Stop looking at wedding blogs!
- I said stop!

Three days to go:

- Take time for yourself. Just you. Even if it's to sit on the couch and stare blankly at a wall.
- Wedding Brain, like Pregnancy Brain, will potentially render you forgetful. I have thus far forgotten my wallet (and thankfully found it), misplaced my sunglasses (and found them), and completely forgotten to pick up our wedding bands. Be kind to yourself, it's almost over.
- You may be just a little emotional. OK. A lot.
- Playing the version of your wedding song the DJ sent to check may render you teary eyed. Enjoy it. And then turn it off and let it go til the night.
- Just remember: "It's just a party with people you love." Great advice given by a friend.
- Now would probably be the time to stop working, if you haven't already.
- Try and take one-on-one time with people coming from abroad.
- Definitely take one-on-one time with your partner. Even if you just stare at the wall together.
- Enjoy that stupid half smile on your face and that funny butterfly excitement feeling.
- Yes, I promise you your period will only come

two days AFTER the wedding. Was there ever any doubt?

- If it's too hard to do now, it's most likely not important. Focus on what can be done. And if possible, get someone you trust to do it.
- It's also your parents' and his parents' wedding.
- It's most likely a little too late to elope.
- Alcohol and wise people in your life are your friends.
- Your husband-to-be is a very special person— thoughtful, wonderful, loving. And he pretends to remember all your friends.

Two days to go:

- Hangover. (Post-bachelorette party.)
- Remember, alcohol should not be mixed. (I was sure I'd learned this lesson before!)
- Take time out for yourself. (I just sat on the couch and vegetated for two hours. I would take more if I could.)
- Sorry, Mom. Bridezilla is under wraps but I still get stressed by things you say.
- Nervous. Anxious. Stressed. Check. Check. Check.
- Thankful I booked yoga tomorrow.
- Loving my friends. Really. Just loving them.

One day to go:

- Strange calm (with butterflies).
- Early morning wake-ups (not the norm).
- Great phone calls and love shower continues.

- Yoga today was an awesome idea!
- Everything is going to be amazing and wonderful.
- Yes, yes, of course you are still stressed.
- Sending a special blessing to the god of clear, glowing skin to shine on you.
- You do not have enough vases for the flowers people are sending you.
- Food is not particularly interesting, but you are keeping hydrated. Keep hydrated!
- That stupid happy smile appears often.
- Everything is going to be alright (a deep knowing has settled over you).
- Don't worry, everything is under control, and your friends and family are going to make it amazing with you.
- Nothing is important except the two of you being there on the day. Really, nothing else. Definitely not tablecloths.
- Apparently four of your friends have glue guns and know how to use them.

The night before, 12:12 am:

- Remembering how helpful the lesson was: "If it's too hard, find an easier way; or drop it off the list; it's not that important."
- Love.
- All emotions at once, mostly butterflies, excitement, wee bit of stress-nervousness-anticipation, lots of love, inner calm and friendship.

- My family and friends are awesome.
- OMG!!!!! It's so freaking soon!!
- Try and get sleep.

7 am—wake up . . .

- Rush around.
- Override "OMG he cut the bottom of his pants and attempted to hem!" with "How cute he was sitting, sewing his own buttons for his suspenders and hemming his pants himself."
- Sit down.
- Stand up.
- Clean house (you can appreciate why people stay in hotels).
- Lots of butterflies and nervous energy.
- Not sure if you are meant to stay a night apart . . . we went with what was most convenient and in the end sleeping together was.
- Yup, still a bundle of energy—mixture of nerves and smiles and laughs and chatter and just a TON of anticipation.
- Now a friend comes with coffeeeeeeeeeeeeeeeeee.

I promise it's going to be magical and fantastic!

"The best thing about being post-wedding is never having to look at another wedding blog again."

— MY FRIEND

The Bride Wore Black

"I can't end this with a wedding."

"Why not?"

"Because it goes against what I stand for."

"Well, maybe you can end it with a non-wedding, or a proposal . . ." offers a girlfriend.

"No," I sigh, "it's been done to death. *Four Weddings and A Funeral, She's Just Not That Into You* . . ."

"OK, um . . ."

So I've invited some friends over for a focus-group-and-lots-of-food-and-wine to discuss what-next's.

"To be honest, darling," one friend interrupts, "maybe you should just move on from endings and focus on some other aspect?"

"Um . . . no thanks . . . but maybe I'll ask a better question. OK guys, what's your favorite type of ending?"

"I actually hate the happily-ever-after ones. Who do you know who's actually that happy?" groans one of the girls.

"Well, actually, I am," one of the other girls jumps in.

"But I agree that it'd be a shame to end with a regular 'and they lived happily ever after' moment," she says.

"What about a Bollywood scene? You can have lots of dancing . . ." someone suggests.

"But that's basically a wedding scene, isn't it?" another friend cuts her off.

"See, it's not that easy" I say.

"Maybe we should just focus on cutting that cake . . ." I motion to the double chocolate cake from Best Ever Bakery that's been staring at us from under the glass cake dish.

Eight nods.

"I'm glad we can achieve consensus on one thing."

"Grrrr," I groan.

"Why are we always eating, drinking, or talking about guys?

I mean, once you have a guy and a few kids, what do people talk about?"

"Nothing, the weather, how many diapers they've changed, sore nipples, what was on the news . . . their few single friends' lives. Oh, and who's getting divorced or cheating," sighs one of the girls.

"Do you know what my friends said the other night at dinner?" asks one of my single girlfriends.

"She said, 'Please don't get married. We'll never have anything to talk about and no good stories.' Like, gee, thanks for rooting for me."

"Ah, that's an interesting chapter. Do couple friends actually want us to be in a couple?" I ask, and jot the question down.

"Or do they prefer to be smug?" slurs one of the girls.

(In her defense, we have had a lot of alcohol by now.)

"But, you *are* in a couple," I say.

"Yeah, but we're not smug. And I remember being unmarried! We were together forever and people used to be like, 'Oh, you're not married yet?'"

Smug.

Smug.

Smug.

"Marriage is about being able to wear your retainers at night, that's all."

— LEANDRA MEDINE,
MANREPELLER.COM

Natalie Shell is an Aussie thinker, storyteller, and coach. In addition to spurting chick lit, she's one half of Apartmentdiet.com; ex-Product Manager, Branding, and UX Junkie at Wix.com; and a former Change Consultant. She lives in Tel Aviv with her Mr. and their son. Previously thought to be immune, she caught and survived the wedding virus.

Stay Tuned

Congratulations...
If you just got married the answer you now need is:

*"No, we're not ready for kids yet,
we're just enjoying being married."*

**In 2016 Natalie Shell will be back
with *The Baby Epidemic*.**

www.thebabyepidemic.com